AFROPUFFS

Power to the Puffs

To: Evan

Enjoy!

Stephanie
Shireman

For Faramola, Ojurere, and
Mojuba

ISBN 978-1-4243-2697-6   2007 Printing

AFROPUFFS

Power to the Puffs

by Stephanie Shonekan

Chapter 1:
Two New Girls

There were two new girls in the fourth grade when classes resumed at University Elementary School in August of 2006. Most of the other students had been at University Elementary since they were in kindergarten.

There were two fourth-grade classes. The children assigned to 4An were excited because everybody in Bloomington, Indiana, knew that Mrs. Anderson was the best teacher at University Elementary School. That is what the 4An children were telling the 4Ba children who were entering Mrs. Ball's classroom across the hall.

Mrs. Anderson was younger than most of the kids' parents. She had bright blonde hair and wore shiny pink lip gloss. On the first day of school, she stood at the door and welcomed each member of her new fourth-grade class. She had been a substitute teacher at this school for a while and knew most of the children well. Now that she had her own class, she was happy to welcome each of them by name.

"Hello, Tom," she smiled at a burly boy who gazed at her speechlessly with admiration. He smiled back and went into the classroom.

Mrs. Anderson spotted another student. "Good morning, Caroline. Did you have a good summer?"

The pretty girl who was wearing a pretty pink dress replied, "Yes, Mrs. Anderson. We went to our beach house." Caroline kept her nose up as if the ground was stinky.

"How nice," Mrs. Anderson said. She knew that Caroline would be eager to go in and let everybody see her new hairstyle and dress. She was a girl who liked attention. "Well, go on in and find a seat." Caroline walked elegantly into the room, a wave of flowery perfume trailing her.

"Welcome, Li," Mrs. Anderson said gently to the shy Chinese boy wearing glasses. He mumbled "Hello," and rushed into the classroom.

The children continued to arrive. Then Mrs. Anderson spotted a new face. "Good morning," she said to a girl with deep brown eyes and two round afropuffs on top of her head. The girl had a serious expression on her face.

"Are you Mrs. Anderson?" she asked solemnly.

"Yes I am," replied Mrs. Anderson. "Are you Zora?"

The girl frowned. Her face grew even more serious. "No," she said shortly.

Mrs. Anderson kept smiling at her. "You must be Makeba then."

The frown disappeared. "Yes. Who is Zora?" Makeba asked.

"That would be me!" A cheerful voice responded, and both Mrs. Anderson and Makeba turned to see a beautiful dark brown girl with a very white smile and a tiny dimple on each cheek. Makeba's eyes widened as she looked at Zora's hair. She also wore her hair in two afropuffs.

Mrs. Anderson looked from one girl to the other. If Makeba were a few shades darker, they would look like twins. Mrs. Anderson said, "Hello, Zora. Welcome, both of you, to University Elementary School."

Makeba nodded and went into the classroom. Zora smiled and said "Thank you," and also went to find her desk in the now-noisy classroom.

All the children, except the two new girls, were chatting with the friends they had not seen all summer. Caroline was telling two girls about her beach house. Several other students nearby were also listening to her loud story. Zora and Makeba found themselves sitting next to each other in the front row. They had no friends in the class because they were both new to the school.

Zora smiled at her neighbor but there was no response, so she shrugged and looked around happily at everybody else in the class.

Then Mrs. Anderson came in and hushed the class. She welcomed the students to section 4An and told them that she had two main ground rules.

"If someone else is speaking, you should listen and not talk too, OK?"

Everybody, even the serious new girl, nodded and waited for Mrs. Anderson's second rule: "Respect each other. Whether we are in this classroom, in the gym, in the lunchroom, or on the playground, I expect everyone to be respected, whether they're from Bloomington, China, or Chi-town." Mrs. Anderson winked at Makeba and for the first time the serious girl smiled. Makeba wondered how her new teacher had found out she was from Chicago. Mrs. Anderson noticed the new smile and knew she had started to break the ice with Makeba.

Chapter 2:
Caroline and Her Girls

"What kind of name is Makeeeba?" The fourth-graders were all in the playground when this question came from the long-haired Caroline in the pink dress. The two girls with her nodded, agreeing with their leader.

Makeba, who had been sitting by herself on a bench reading a book, looked up. "It's an African name. And it's Ma-kay-ba, not Makeeeba."

"Whatever! It sure is strange!" Caroline said. The other girls giggled.

Zora, who had been walking around the playground watching the groups of friends play, had stopped near the bench to listen. "It is a beautiful name," she said.

"What do *you* know?" one of Caroline's girls, Janelle, asked. Caroline nodded at Janelle, who had the same hairstyle and fashion as Caroline. The only difference was that she had brown skin and a blue dress. Like Caroline, Janelle was looking at Zora and Makeba as if they were aliens.

"It is the name of a great African singer, Miriam Makeba," said Zora.

"Is she one of those rappers?" Caroline asked with a smirk on her face and her nose in the air.

Zora and Makeba looked at each other and giggled. Makeba looked pretty when she laughed, thought Zora.

"What's so funny?" asked Julie, Caroline's other friend, whose brown hair matched her brown freckles. She looked really curious.

"Miriam Makeba is probably as old as your grandmother!" said Makeba.

"So?" Caroline stepped back.

"So, does your grandmother listen to rap music?" Makeba asked.

Caroline was annoyed because now her girls, Julie and Janelle, were giggling too. She glared at them so they stopped laughing but they could not help smiling.

Caroline turned toward Zora. "Besides, *you* have a strange accent."

"So do you," said Zora cheerfully.

Caroline kept going, wanting to win points against these two new girls. "Where are you from anyway? Mars?" She looked at her girls and they laughed obediently.

"No. Pluto. You don't see my horns?" replied Zora with a big smile. Makeba became pretty again as she threw her head back and howled with laughter.

Caroline huffed and puffed and spun on her heel. She told her girls to follow her, they were going to the bathroom. Off they went.

"Thanks for helping me out with those three," said Makeba.

Zora shrugged. "You really have a beautiful name."

"Thanks. My mom is so proud of the name. She loves Africa. My younger brother is named Mandela. We call him Manny."

"Wow," said Zora. "You know who I was named after?"

"Who?"

"Zora Neale Hurston. My mother's favorite writer was called Zora Neale Hurston."

"That's awesome," said Makeba. "What part of Pluto are you from?" She smiled as she asked the question.

"From Nigeria."

"West Africa," said Makeba. "I can tell you where all the countries in Africa are."

"You're better than me. All I know is where Nigeria is."

"How come?" asked Makeba. She was surprised that an African did not know much about the continent.

Zora shrugged. "I don't know. Not that interested."

"What do your parents do?"

"It's just me and my mother. She just got a job here at Indiana University. She's a writer. She teaches literature, fiction." Zora laughed. "It gets complicated. We used to live in Washington, DC, where my mom went to school. We just moved here."

"Me too!" Makeba exclaimed. "My mother just moved us here from Chicago. She is a professor too. Anthropology."

"An-thro-what?" asked Zora.

"An-thro-po-lo-gy," said Makeba.

Zora laughed. "Sounds complicated too."

"Not really," said Makeba. "She gets to study African cultures."

"Oh," said Zora. "Sounds too serious."

"Hmmm." Makeba wondered about this other new girl. She did not seem to take anything very seriously.

"Where do you live?" asked Zora, sure that she had found her first friend.

"Redbud Apartments, on the college campus," replied Makeba.

Zora clapped her hands excitedly. "Oh good. I live in Tulip Tree Apartments. Not far from you."

The two girls were amazed at how much they had in common. They looked around at all the different groups on the playground. Some boys were tossing a ball around. A group of girls was playing with a jump rope. Caroline and her girls had come back from the bathroom looking neat and pretty. They were talking and laughing. Only the quiet boy with glasses, Li, was sitting by himself, under a tree, reading a book.

Makeba supposed she could like this happy Zora. "Seems like we have a lot in common, Miss Hurston. We should hang out."

"Yes. We should."

Chapter 3:

Grumpy and Happy

The following day, Zora took the school bus for the first time, and she found herself on the same bus as Makeba. They were delighted. They could not sit next to each other because by the time the bus got to Zora's stop, Makeba was already sitting next to her first-grade brother, Manny.

As soon as they got off the bus in front of the school, the two girls got together and arranged to save seats for each other on the bus from then on.

"Manny will just have to sit with some other snotty-nosed first-grader" Makeba said. The good thing was that Manny had already made friends with a little boy next door called Georgie who had shiny straight black hair and skin the color of peanut butter. Georgie was also in first grade. On

the way home after school, Manny sat with him
and Zora got to sit with Makeba.

The first couple of weeks went really well for
Zora and Makeba. People at school got used to
seeing the two girls together. Caroline and her girls
started calling them "Grumpy and Happy" because
the one with the strange name was so serious,
always frowning, and the one with the accent was
so cheerful, always smiling.

"Here come Grumpy and Happy," Caroline
would say loudly when the girls walked past. Pretty
soon, the rest of the kids in the class started calling
them that too.

Mrs. Anderson heard it and was going to put a stop to it. But she decided not to say anything when she saw how well Makeba and Zora handled it. The two girls ignored Caroline and her girls most of the time.

Makeba and Zora were alike in some ways, but very different too. Zora's favorite subjects were math and music. Makeba liked social studies best. When it was time for math, Zora would get her work done quickly and take it to Mrs. Anderson. Makeba would just doodle on her book, so she would always be the last to get her math done. When the music teacher, Mr. Frist, asked for volunteers to sing, Zora jumped up first. She had a sweet voice. Everybody, even Caroline and her girls, liked to hear her sing. Makeba did not like music much because she did not sing well. She never volunteered in class, even though she liked to sing at home.

But then, when it was time for social studies, Makeba's hand was always up, asking questions, answering questions. She knew where all the continents were located on the globe. When it was time to go to the computers and do social studies research in pairs, Zora would sit by Makeba twiddling her thumbs while Makeba's fingers sped across the keyboard.

"Here come the dwarfs," said Caroline to Julie one afternoon in the playground. The girls walked past.

Zora looked confused. She turned to her friend. "We are both taller than Caroline, so why is she calling us dwarfs?"

Makeba gave one of her rare smiles. "Because Happy and Grumpy are two of Snow White's dwarfs. Don't you know that fairy tale?"

"Oh yes," said Zora. "I just did not know what the dwarfs' names were."

"Yeah. Forget about Caroline. She'll stop picking on us when she realizes we don't care."

"You know, Makeba," said Zora. "If you smiled more, they would stop calling you Grumpy."

Makeba looked back at Caroline and her girls. Janelle was busy fixing the blue ribbon in Caroline's hair.

"Nah. I like that they call me Grumpy," she said. "My mother says they won't mess with me if they think I'm baaad."

"And my mother says not everybody has to like me," Zora said. "OK. As long as you don't mind. Come on. Let's go play jump rope over there."

Chapter 4:

The Wise Old Man

One afternoon, there was much excitement in the playground. Everybody was gathered around Tom, the big boy in 4An. He was arranging a race.

"Can we run too?" asked Zora.

Tom looked around at some of the other boys. They nodded because they knew that both Makeba and Zora were fast.

"OK. You can be a team leader," Tom said, pointing at Zora. "Jerry, Bob, and I are the other team leaders. We're going to run a relay race, four runners in each team. So we'll take turns picking our teams, OK?"

Zora said, "OK. I pick my girl Makeba."

Makeba smiled and stood behind Zora. The other three team leaders picked their first team members. They picked only boys.

Then it was Zora's turn again. "Let's see. I pick Julie." Julie was Caroline's girl with freckles. She jumped behind Makeba before Caroline could stop her. Zora had seen her run in PE and knew she was fast.

There was only one spot left on Zora's team when it was her turn again. She looked around the playground. Makeba whispered, "I guess you have to pick Katie."

Zora was about to call Katie when her eyes met Li's. The quiet boy who always sat by himself reading quickly looked down.

"I pick Li," said Zora loudly.

"What?" Makeba whispered. "*He* can't run."

Zora whispered back, "We don't know that. We've never seen him run."

"We'll lose," said Makeba. All the other kids snickered as Li put his book down and walked over to stand behind Julie.

Katie called, "On your marks, get set, go!" The first four contestants ran across the schoolyard and touched the chosen tree, then came back to touch the next person on their team. Then the second group of four did the same. Zora's team and Tom's team were leading until Julie fell down. By the time she got up again, their team was coming in last.

Then she touched Li and he took off. The whole
playground watched, amazed. Li, holding his
glasses in one hand, ran to the tree as if he were
flying. He flew past the other three runners and
came back to Zora before any of the others. Zora's
team won.

"Wow, Li!" Makeba said. "I didn't think you
could run like that!"

He put his glasses back on. "Why not?"

She stuttered. "Well, because you're so quiet and
all you do is read. You always have a book."

He smiled and said wisely, "Ah. You cannot judge a book…"

"…by its cover." Both Zora and Makeba finished the sentence.

He nodded and replied, "And you cannot get the fortune message until you crack the fortune cookie open."

Makeba laughed. "You are a wise old man, Li." The girls had just made a new friend.

Chapter 5:
The Club

The school gym was crowded with parents and students on a Friday afternoon. Mrs. Anderson had sent letters home the day before. All the girls got letters about Girl Scouts and all the boys got letters about Boy Scouts. Today, the parents were invited back to school to sign the girls and boys up for the troops.

Both Makeba and Zora wanted to be Girl Scouts, so their mothers were among the crowd in the gym that afternoon.

Of course Caroline and her girls were there with their mothers. They were already signed up. They had been in the same troop since they were Daisies in kindergarten.

Since Makeba and Zora were new, they had a

lot more paperwork to fill out. While Makeba's mother, Kim, and Zora's mother, Chika, went to the table to get the forms, Makeba and Zora went to see what the other girls were doing.

"What are Grumpy and Happy doing here?" Caroline asked loudly.

Julie answered quietly, "Just leave them alone, alright?" She did not like picking on Makeba and Zora all the time. Sometimes, they looked like they were having so much more fun than Caroline and her girls.

"What's up with you?" Janelle asked Julie.

Julie shrugged and was quiet. Makeba and Zora sat with some of the older girls who were showing off some photos.

After a while the girls went over to see what their mothers were doing. Makeba's mother, Kim, looked at the paperwork. "Girl," exclaimed Kim to Chika. "These are a lot of forms to fill."

"I know. Doctor's phone number; health insurance number … I hope I have all the information they need," Chika replied, digging through her bag to pull out cards.

After they had turned in the forms, the Girl Scout troop leader, who also happened to be Julie's mother, introduced herself.

"Any questions?" she asked.

"Yes," said Kim immediately. "What day and time do the girls meet?"

The leader replied, "Every other Friday at 5 p.m. We meet over at my house in the subdivision behind the school."

After the meeting, Makeba and Zora got into the back of Chika's car. Kim got into the passenger side.

As Chika drove them all back to the campus, Kim asked her, "Could you bring the girls to their meetings on those days?"

"I was going to ask you the same question. I teach a class on Friday till 6 o'clock," Chika said.

"And my students' Culture Club meets on Friday evenings. I'm their faculty advisor so I have to be there," Kim said with a frown.

Makeba and Zora looked at each other, worried. "Does this mean we can't be Girl Scouts?" asked Makeba, a frown appearing on her forehead, so that she looked just like her mother.

"Well," said Kim, turning back to look at the girls, "It means that it will be difficult to get you girls to and from the meetings."

The girls looked crestfallen. The two mothers looked at their daughters. They both looked so sad.

"I have an idea," said Kim. "The girls can join my anthropology students' club. I'm sure the college students wouldn't mind. They do some really fun and interesting stuff."

The two girls looked uncertain. Chika liked the idea. "Ah-ha. So they will have a club of their own?" she exclaimed.

"Exactly," said Kim. "Every other Friday, or every Friday if they like, the girls can come with me to the Culture Club meetings on campus."

"But why can't we be Girl Scouts?" Makeba whined.

"Give it a chance, Makeba," her mother replied. "The anthropology students are great. You will both love this club. I can guarantee it."

Zora started getting excited. "Wow. We'll meet with college students?"

Chika laughed at her daughter's excitement. "Do you know what anthropology is?"

Zora tried to remember what *anthro-* meant. "Culture? How different people live?"

"Good girl," said Chika. They were driving up to Redbud Apartments, where Kim and Makeba lived. "How did you know that?" Chika asked her daughter.

"Makeba told me."

"Good girl," Kim smiled at her daughter.

"What do they do at the meetings?" asked Makeba, beginning to like the idea.

"They meet to talk about their anthropology research. They share ideas. They talk about their fieldwork."

"Fieldwork?" asked Zora.

"Yes. Fieldwork is like . . . detective work, getting information so you can learn something about a culture." Kim looked hopefully at the girls. "So we'll give it a try?"

"Only if we get to do fieldwork too," Makeba said, the crease in her forehead beginning to disappear now as a smile slowly crept across her face.

Kim thought about it for a minute. She looked at Chika. "OK. That might work. The college students in the club will teach you two how to do fieldwork, and you can do some research on campus."

"Awesome!" The girls were both excited.

Chapter 6:

Embrace the Puffs

Julie stopped Makeba and Zora as they were passing the lunch table where she sat with Caroline and Janelle. As usual, Caroline was in a pretty dress and her two lieutenants were close beside her.

Julie said, "So you two aren't joining our Girl Scout troop? My mom said you weren't joining us after all." Julie had looked forward to hanging out with Makeba and Zora.

"Oh?" This came from Caroline. "No Girl Scouts for you?" She looked happy.

"Nope," replied Zora happily. "Sorry to disappoint you." Her dimples were floating around on her cheeks.

"Too bad. We'll be thinking about you when

we're having fun at our meetings," Caroline said gleefully.

"And we'll think about *you* when we're enjoying our meetings," Zora replied.

Caroline looked surprised. Janelle too. "What meetings?" Janelle asked.

Makeba tossed her head back. She linked her arm in Zora's. "Come on, Zora. Time for lunch."

"Hey," Caroline called after them. "Why don't you two do something with your hair?"

"Why?" Makeba frowned. "What's wrong with our hair?" She touched one of her afropuffs proudly.

Caroline looked at the puffs disdainfully. "Well, they make you look like Mickey Mouse. I'm sure if you ask Janelle nicely, she'll tell you what to do to straighten it out. Right, Janelle?"

Janelle ran her fingers through her straight hair. "No problem."

Zora reached over and touched Janelle's hair. "Nice, I suppose, if that's what you like," Zora said. "But I like my hair as it is."

Janelle said, "Your mom won't let you straighten your hair, right? My mom let me straighten mine when I was in kindergarten. Makes life easier. And it's prettier too."

"That is your opinion, Janelle," Makeba said. Then she turned to Caroline. "You want to touch the puffs, don't you, Caroline?"

Caroline hissed. "No, I do not!"

"Yes you do. The puffs have some hidden powers," said Makeba in a mysterious voice. Caroline looked suspicious. Makeba laughed and pulled on Zora's hand. They went off to sit with Li.

They began to unpack their lunch boxes. "Maybe they're right, Makeba," said Zora.

"Right about what?" asked Li, biting into a carrot.

"About our hair. Maybe we should tell our mothers to let us straighten it like Janelle's."

Makeba frowned. "I asked her when I was in first grade and she said no."

"Me too," said Zora. "Makeba, maybe we should ask them again."

Li chewed on his carrot thoughtfully for a minute. "Don't you like your hair as it is?" he asked finally after he had swallowed.

"Actually, I do," said Makeba. "It makes me look like me."

"And I don't really want to look like Janelle," said Zora. She giggled at the thought.

"Then why do you want to let Caroline tell you not to like those cute puffs?" Li asked.

Zora and Makeba looked at each other. Li was right. Makeba picked up her sandwich. "Besides, when did we start taking beauty advice from Caroline?"

"Maybe we can get a different hairstyle, without the straightener," Zora said, biting into her apple.

"My mom doesn't know how to braid. Can your mom braid?" Makeba asked Zora.

Zora nodded and sighed at the same time. "Yes. She used to do lovely hairstyles for me. With beads and ribbons. But now that she's a professor, she never has time to do anything different to my hair. So I'm left with the afropuffs."

"Embrace the puffs," said Li, the wise old man, and the three of them laughed heartily. By the end of lunch time, the girls had agreed to embrace the puffs. They would love their hair. They would not ask their mothers about straightening it right now, they agreed. At least not until fifth grade.

Chapter 7:

The First Meeting

The two girls were nervous and excited when they went with Kim to the anthropology students' Culture Club meeting on Friday evening. The group called themselves the Culture Club because they were all studying different cultures.

"There are cultures all around us," Carlos, one of the students, told the girls. "So we call ourselves the Culture Club!"

Makeba and Zora sat at the round table with the college students listening to what they were saying. Everyone was munching on the plantain chips that Carlos had brought to the meeting.

There were seven students, all members of the Culture Club. They were discussing the different things they were doing in their ethnographies. Kim explained to the girls that "ethnography" was a word that meant describing people.

She asked the students to start by telling the girls what people and cultures they were studying. Kim told the girls to take notes in the little notebooks she had bought them. So the girls wrote their lists:

-David: Music in Peru (Zora liked that!)

-Karla: Native American jewelry making

-Brian: Fiddling in Canada

-Jeff: Cambodian religion --(Zora had no idea where Cambodia was. Makeba knew exactly where it was.)

-Carlos: Africans in Brazil (Interesting, both girls noted.)

-Tatiana: Women in South Africa (Makeba put a star next to this one.)

-Laura: Basketball culture in Bloomington

Makeba's hand went up when the last student to speak, Laura, said she was studying basketball culture in Bloomington. "Right here in Bloomington, Indiana? Don't you have to go away to do anthropology research?"

"Not always," replied the quiet Laura. "There are cultures everywhere in the world, even here in Bloomington."

"Wow," both girls said.

34

Kim asked the students to go around the table and tell the girls one thing they had to know to do good fieldwork.

"Take notes, girls," Kim said.

-*Carlos: Ask lots of questions.*

-*Tatiana: Study before you ask questions. Be patient.*

-*Brian: Make notes, lots of notes.*

-*David: Record with a tape recorder, but ask first.*

-*Karla: Study from a distance. Don't get involved!*

-*Jeff: Remember you are not better than the people you are studying.*

-*Laura: Be observant. Study the culture around you. That's why we are called the Culture Club.*

Laura seemed to always be the last to speak. The meeting went on and the girls listened quietly. Brian played some fiddle music he had collected in Canada over the summer. Carlos showed photos of Brazilians. The girls were amazed to see that there were so many different colors of people in Brazil.

Then Carlos asked the girls what project they would be working on. They shrugged because they did not know yet. Laura had said there was culture everywhere, so they knew they could find something close by to study.

Kim chuckled. "They'll find something, I'm sure. They will tell us about what they come up with the next time they visit."

Chapter 8:

Finding a Project

The girls brainstormed for days on what they wanted to study for their Culture Club project. They could not agree on anything.

"Should we study the culture of Caroline and her girls?" Zora asked jokingly at school one day.

"Never!" Makeba frowned. "Then they'll know what we're doing."

"Maybe we should ask Mrs. Anderson," Zora said to Makeba.

"Good idea. She always knows what to do."

When the class was excused for recess, the two girls waited to make sure they were the only ones left. Then they went up to Mrs. Anderson's desk. They told her about their club.

"That's wonderful, girls!" their teacher

exclaimed. "I can't wait to hear what your ethnography is going to be about."

"Well, that's the thing," Zora said. "We don't know what to do. Can you help?"

Mrs. Anderson thought for a few moments. "I belong to a women's book club. Would you like to study us?"

The girls looked hopeful. "Oh," said Makeba. "That might work. Do you guys read mysteries?"

Mrs. Anderson laughed and shook her head. "No. We read biographies. Stories about people's lives. Sometimes we read fiction."

"That sounds interesting," said Zora. "We could study who the women are in this book club. See if they all like the books they are reading."

"Yeah, the culture of book clubs," said Makeba, liking the idea. "Can we come to your meeting?"

"I'll have to ask the ladies," replied Mrs. Anderson. "But I'm sure they wouldn't mind."

"Good. When do you meet?" asked Makeba getting out her Culture Club notebook.

"Next month on the third Saturday."

"Oh." The girls' shoulders fell because that was way too far away. They really wanted something to report to the Culture Club meeting next week. They had to do at least some work on their project before

then. This book club meeting of Mrs. Anderson's was too far in the future.

"Problem?" asked Mrs. Anderson. The girls explained why they had to find something else. They were still talking to Mrs. Anderson when Caroline and her girls walked in.

"What's up?" asked Caroline, smiling at Mrs. Anderson. She really wanted to know what these two were up to. She did not like to be left out of anything.

Before Mrs. Anderson could answer, Makeba said, "Oh, nothing much." Mrs. Anderson understood immediately that Makeba and Zora had found themselves a cool club and did not want to share it with anyone, at least not right now. Mrs. Anderson decided to keep their secret.

Out in the playground, Li saw his two friends coming out of the building with sad expressions on their faces. He stopped playing tag with Tom and the other boys and came over to talk to them. He did not play much but now that the kids knew how fast he could run, they were always asking him to play with them.

"Why the long faces, Afropuffs?" he asked. He had started calling them that ever since their talk about hair.

"We can't find anything to study for our Culture Club project," said Makeba.

"Why not? There is so much around to choose from."

"Like what?" asked Zora.

"You two live on a college campus. There are a lot of students and professors there from around the world. Surely you could study a neighbor?" he asked.

Makeba's eyes lit up. "I know just the people!"

"Who?" Zora and Li asked together.

"You know Manny's little friend? The one he sits with on the bus?"

40

Zora nodded. "Georgie?"

"Mm-hmm. Does he look African to you?"

"Not really," mused Zora. "I mean, his skin is sort of brown but his hair looks Indian. I thought he was Indian or Pakistani or something."

"He says he's African."

"What do his parents look like?" Li asked.

"His dad looks Indian," Makeba said slowly. "But his mother, I don't really know."

"What do you mean?" asked Zora.

"I've never seen her," Makeba explained. "She always stays inside."

"Who brings him to the bus?"

"His dad."

"Well, we need to find out why she stays in and why Georgie thinks he's African."

"A good project," said Li.

Chapter 9:

A Few Questions

The girls checked their notes from the first Culture Club meeting. "Ask lots of questions" was the first thing on the list. So the next day, after school, they sat outside Redbud Apartments watching Manny and Georgie riding their bikes on the pavement.

"Hey Manny, Georgie," Makeba called. "Come over here."

"What for?" asked Manny as he zoomed past.

"We want to ask you some questions," Zora said, motioning to the boys to come over.

"We don't want to talk to girls," Manny shouted back.

"OK then," Makeba said. "I guess Zora and I are going inside and that means you have to come

inside too. You know Mom said you could only be outside if we're here with you." The girls got up and pretended to go inside.

"OK, OK. What do you want to ask?" Manny and Georgie rode over and stopped in front of the girls.

"Where are you from, Georgie?" Zora asked smiling at the little boys.

"Africa," was his one-word response.

"So am I," she said patiently. "I'm from Nigeria."

The two boys looked at her with blank expressions on their faces.

"Where in Africa are you from, Georgie?" Makeba asked trying to be patient. That was one of the rules in her notebook.

"Kenya," Georgie said. "Now can we go riding?"

"Sure," Zora said. The boys rushed off.

Makeba frowned at her friend. "Why did you let them go? I wanted to ask him about his mother."

"Well, now that we know where he's from, we can do some research first." Zora opened her notebook and carefully wrote out the word, "Kenya."

Makeba nodded. "All right. We can do our research in the library at school tomorrow."

Chapter 10:
Crazy Club!

The following day, Makeba and Zora asked Mrs. Anderson if they could do some of their Culture Club research during the library hour. There were lots of computers in the library and this would be a good time to get some information on Kenya.

"As long as you save time to return your library books and check some more out, that's fine," whispered Mrs. Anderson. Caroline was still snooping around them trying to figure out what they were up to.

As soon as they got to the library, Makeba and Zora rushed through the shelves, found some books on Africa and put them aside so that they could check them out. Then they sat at the computer, Makeba at the keyboard and Zora standing next to

her taking notes in her notebook.

-Kenya is in East Africa.

-They speak several languages, including English and Swahili.

-Safari

"The safari sounds like fun," Zora said.

"Mmm," mumbled Makeba as she continued to search on the Internet. "That still doesn't explain why Georgie *thinks* he's Kenyan. I still say he's Indian."

"Why don't you do a search with the words

'Indian' and 'Kenya'?" Zora suggested.

"Good idea," said Makeba. She typed in the words.

"Red alert," whispered Zora as she spotted Caroline coming up behind them. By the time Caroline got there, Makeba had pulled up the library catalog page on the computer screen so that Caroline could not tell what they were doing.

"What are you two up to?" she asked with her eyes squinting at the screen.

"Same thing you should be doing," Makeba replied. "Looking for books to check out."

"I'm watching you, Makeeeba." Caroline insisted on pronouncing her name wrong and Makeba had stopped trying to correct her. Caroline huffed off.

Makeba went back to her search page and clicked on an article. "This looks interesting but time is almost up," she said, glancing up at the big round clock on the library wall.

"Print it out and we can read it at home," Zora said. So Makeba sent it to print and logged off the computer. By the time the two girls got to the printer, Caroline and her girls were standing there reading their article!

"Give us that!" Makeba shouted.

"Shhh," the librarian looked over her glasses at them with a finger over her mouth.

"Can we have our article please?" Zora whispered pleasantly.

"Well, what do we have here?" Janelle looked over Caroline's shoulder.

Caroline folded the article and walked out of the library followed by her girls and Makeba and Zora close behind. She headed for their classroom. Mrs. Anderson was at her desk getting ready for the next lesson. When she saw the five girls walk in, she knew there was trouble.

"Give us that back, right now," said Makeba.

"Oh stop being so grumpy," Caroline said as she sat on the edge of a desk and looked at the pages. "People of Kenya? Where is that?"

"Pluto," said Zora nicely.

Caroline rolled her eyes at Zora. "What's this about?" she asked, annoyed. "Is there a class assignment I need to know about? If you don't tell me, I'll throw this away."

Makeba looked toward Mrs. Anderson. "Mrs. Anderson, could you tell this girl to give us back our research?"

"Caroline, do you have something that doesn't belong to you?" asked Mrs. Anderson gently.

"It was just on the printer. It could've been anyone's." Caroline thrust the article at Zora.

"Girls," said Mrs. Anderson, putting her pen down. "Maybe it's time to tell the others about your cool club."

Makeba shrugged silently, her arms folded stubbornly over her chest.

"We are in an anthropology club and we are studying Kenyans," Zora explained briefly.

"Is that what you're doing instead of Girl Scouts?" Julie asked.

"Yes, our mothers could not bring us out to your troop meetings on Fridays so we decided to join a different club."

"I could ask my mother if she can pick you up on Fridays for the Scout troop," Julie said hopefully.

Zora smiled at her. She thought Julie was actually much nicer than Caroline and Janelle. "Thanks, Julie. We'll stick with our anthropology club now. We actually enjoy it."

"What's *anpolology* anyway?" Caroline asked smugly.

Makeba was quick to correct her. "Anthropology. We study world cultures."

Caroline wrinkled her nose. "What good is that?"

51

"Oh, Caroline," said Mrs. Anderson. "It's good to learn about other people. You learn a lot about yourself when you learn about others."

Caroline smiled sweetly at Mrs. Anderson and walked back to her desk. As she passed Makeba, she mumbled, "Sounds like a crazy club to me!"

Chapter 11:

Meeting Mr. Patel

At the next Culture Club meeting, the girls told the group what they had chosen to do for their project. They read from their notebooks and said they had found out that lots of Indians live in Kenya.

"Why is that?" asked Carlos. Kim and the other students looked at Makeba and Zora, waiting for a reply.

"Umm," said Zora. "We don't know really. We just know that there are lots of Indians there."

Kim nodded. "OK. So Georgie really can call himself African, right? Now when you do your fieldwork, you should ask questions about why Indians live in Kenya, OK?"

The two girls nodded and then Makeba said,

"And we want to find out why Georgie's mom never comes out of the apartment."

"Hmm," Kim thought for a moment. "Isn't that a bit personal? Should that be part of the project? What do the other club members think?" She invited the others to respond.

Karla, the stern woman who was studying Native American jewelry, said, "I think the girls just need to ask questions about Kenyan Indians. Ask about their customs. No need to find out about the mother." The girls remembered it was Karla who had given them the *"Don't get involved"* rule.

The quiet Laura who was working on the cool basketball culture project disagreed. "I think," she said slowly—she always spoke slowly. "I think they *should* find out about why the mother stays inside. That might show them some more about the culture."

There was some discussion. In the end, the club advised the girls to proceed carefully.

"Ask good questions!" said Karla forcefully.

"But remember not to hurt anyone's feelings," Laura said slowly.

The girls took notes and decided they would try to interview the Patels tomorrow since it was Saturday. Then they ate some plantain chips and drank orange pop and listened to how the other projects were going.

Georgie's father, Mr. Patel, drove Georgie and Manny to a friend's birthday party early on Saturday morning. Just before they left, Georgie ran back in to say goodbye to his mother, so the girls knew she was in the apartment. After the boys left, Zora and Makeba went to the Patel's front door. They knocked and waited for someone to come to the door. Nobody came.

Makeba knocked again, even louder this time. They waited, their notebooks in hand. They expected to hear footsteps coming to the door. But still there was no sign of movement.

"Maybe she's sleeping," Zora whispered.

"But Georgie just said goodbye to her," Makeba said in a hushed voice.

They tried again with no success.

"This is strange," said Makeba.

"Creepy," replied Zora. "Maybe she doesn't exist!" They walked back to Makeba's apartment and sat on the steps outside. "Let's watch their window and see if the curtains move," suggested Zora. So they sat and waited for three hours.

By the time Mr. Patel's car pulled back into the parking lot, the girls had decided to ask him some questions.

"Here's your brother," Mr. Patel said as he walked Manny over to the girls. "Tell your mother he had a good time."

"Thank you for taking him," Makeba said politely. "Um, Mr. Patel, can we ask you some questions?"

"Sure," he said immediately.

"Are you Indian or African?" Makeba asked.

He seemed taken aback. He put his hand in his pocket and placed a leg on one of the steps. "A good question. But why do you ask?"

"We are members of an anthropology club and we chose to do our project on Kenya."

"Ah. Interesting. Well, there was a lot of migration by Indians at one time in the first half of the twentieth century."

"Migration?" Zora did not know what that meant.

"Oh, you mean moving from one place to another, right?" asked Makeba.

"Yes," he said smiling.

Zora nodded, understanding. "Like my mother and me—we migrated from Nigeria to the United States."

"Exactly," he agreed. The girls scribbled in their notebooks.

"Ah. But aren't you all still Indian?" Makeba asked.

"Yes," he said. "I suppose I am. But I was born in Kenya so I think of myself first as a Kenyan. There are many of us who do."

The girls scribbled.

Mr. Patel looked at his watch. "I'm sorry, girls. I have to go. If you have any other questions, just catch me at the bus stop, alright?"

"Thank you," both girls called as they watched him hurry to his apartment door.

Then they turned to each other. "Really interesting," said Zora.

"Yes," Makeba replied. "But did you notice how he only talked about himself? What about his wife?"

"Hmm."

Chapter 12:

Help from Julie

Sometime the following week, the girls sat in the playground talking about the different possible answers to the mystery of Mrs. Patel.

"I bet there is no Mrs. Patel," said Makeba. "Maybe the state will take Georgie away if they find out there is no mother in the house."

"Oh I don't think so," Zora said with her hand on her chin. "Georgie talks about his mom a lot. Just this morning on the bus, he said she had packed him a tuna sandwich. And he was trying to trade it for Manny's ham sandwich."

"That's true," Makeba sighed. "And Manny says he has met her before, one time when they went in for a glass of water."

"Really? What did he say about her?"

"He didn't say anything! Boys don't notice anything! All he said was she was a woman. What good is that?"

Li, who had been quietly reading a book on the bench next to them straightened his glasses. "Boys do notice things," he said quietly.

The girls giggled, forgetting about their problem for a minute. "Well, you're different, Li. You're one of us!" Makeba teased him. He smiled.

"We should go and knock on their door until she comes to open it," said Makeba stubbornly.

"No," Li shook his head. "Doesn't your notebook say you should not upset anybody?"

"Yeah. So?" Makeba had both her hands up.

"That sounds like something Caroline would say," Li said.

Her hands came down. "OK. So what should we do?"

"We should talk to Mr. Patel again. Ask him if we can talk to his wife," Zora said. Makeba agreed.

Just then, Julie came up to the bench. She looked behind her to see if her two friends were around. Caroline and Janelle were nowhere in sight.

"Hi," Julie said, pushing aside her dark brown hair that always covered her right eye. "I have something for you." She put her hand in her pocket and pulled out a yellow envelope. She handed it to Zora.

Zora opened it and pulled out five beautiful glossy photographs. "Wow, these are nice!" Zora exclaimed. "Where did you get these?" Makeba looked over at the photos and took them from Zora. There were two photos of giraffes, one of a yawning lion, one of a very colorful bird, and one of a monkey.

Julie smiled. When she smiled, the freckles on her nose crinkled up. "I took them. Photography is my hobby. We went to Disney World last summer and visited the Animal Kingdom. It's all about

Africa, you know."

"Why do you want us to have them?" Makeba asked suspiciously. After all, Julie was one of Caroline's girls.

Julie's smile faltered. "Well, Li told me you were studying Africa for your club and I thought you might like these."

"We do," said Zora, giving Julie one of her biggest smiles. "Thanks." Makeba was about to say something but just then Caroline and Janelle approached. Julie went over to them so that they would not see what was going on. She really did not want them to know about this. They might laugh at her.

Makeba looked at the three girls. "I don't want help from Julie. See? She can't even stand up to that awful Caroline."

"But they are nice photos," said Zora. "We could really use them for our project."

"I don't know…." Makeba was shaking her head.

Li took off his glasses and cleaned them with his ever-present hanky. "Sometimes when you let others help you, you are really helping them," he said slowly.

The girls understood. They admired Julie's photos again.

Makeba and Zora sat at the dining table in Zora's apartment. Zora's mother, Chika, was grading papers and the girls were making their anthropology display board. Since every other member of the Culture Club brought in photos or music to share with the others at the meeting, the girls had decided to make a board with information and pictures.

Zora handed Makeba the photos Julie had given them. Makeba put some glue on the four corners and carefully placed the photos on the board.

"So how's it going, girls?" Chika asked, taking her reading glasses off and examining their board. "Nice work."

The girls told her what they had learned so far. "Good work. What are those photos on the board?" she asked, putting her glasses back on and reaching up close to look at the board. "Hmmm. Where did these come from? Mr. Patel?"

"No. Julie gave them to us. She likes to take photographs. I guess it's her hobby," said Makeba. "She and her family went to Disney's Animal Kingdom for summer vacation last year."

Chika raised her eyebrows. "Oh? I thought Julie was one of Caroline's girls?"

"Well she is, sort of," Makeba nodded. "But Li convinced us to let her help."

"That little Li is full of old wisdom," Chika laughed.

Zora handed Makeba another photo. "Here's a really cool photo of a giraffe." Makeba began to prepare it for the board.

"But you haven't talked to any giraffes about Kenya, have you?" Chika said with a chuckle.

"Well, no," the girls said, trying to understand her point.

"You're studying the *people* of Kenya, not the *animals*, girls! And Disney's Animal Kingdom is not your field." She folded her hands in front of her and saw that the girls still did not understand what she was trying to say. "What I'm saying is this. We always get these photos of animals when we read about Kenya or Africa. The cool thing about what you are doing is that you are learning about *people*. So get photos of people!"

Zora looked worried. "But, Mama. What about Julie? We will hurt her feelings if we don't use her photos."

"Not if we think of another way she can help," Makeba said.

Chika nodded. "And maybe in the future you can do a project on Disney World visitors." The girls felt better. They began to pull the photos gently off the board.

Chapter 13:
The Mystery
of Mrs. Patel

After school on Friday, the girls waited for Mr. Patel to return home from work. Georgie and Manny were playing video games in Makeba's house. Kim was reading in the living room. So Makeba and Zora sat outside and waited. Georgie had told them that his father would be home at 5 p.m. after his class. So the girls sat and chatted. They wondered what Caroline would say if she knew her girl Julie was trying to help them. And they were wondering what Mr. Patel would say.

When they saw the little green car drive into the parking lot, they took a deep breath and walked over to Mr. Patel.

He got out of the car and reached in for his brown leather bag. He noticed the girls. "Good evening, girls. More questions for me?"

"Yes, please," Makeba responded. "We were wondering if we could meet your wife?"

He stopped smiling and looked at them. "Why?"

"Well, since we are studying Kenya, we want to talk to more than one person about it. And since your wife is Kenyan…." Zora tried to be brave and bright.

"She *is* Kenyan, isn't she?" Makeba added.

For a moment he was silent. Then he put his hand in his pocket. Then he cleared his throat.

"Yes," he said quietly. "She is Kenyan, Makeba."

"Can we meet her?" Makeba asked.

"If it's too much trouble, we won't bother you," Zora hurried to say. She was sensitive, and she had noticed that Mr. Patel was not comfortable.

"No. It's no trouble. Let's sit down for a moment girls." He sat on one of the steps and the two girls sat on either side of him. "I suppose you can talk to her. She does not have a lot of energy. You can't stay too long."

"What's wrong with her? Is she OK?" Makeba asked, looking worried.

"She's ill. I don't know if she'll want to talk to

you. Let me ask her first, all right?"

The girls nodded. Mr. Patel went into his apartment and the girls waited for about five minutes. Then he opened the door and beckoned to the girls to come in.

The first thing they noticed when they entered the apartment was how neat everything was in the living room. Mr. Patel stood at a bedroom door and motioned them toward him. They went in and stopped just inside the bedroom door, for there, in a small bed, sat a small, pretty black woman. She had a scarf on her head.

"Hello," she said and smiled weakly at them. "Which one is Manny's sister?"

"I am," said Makeba. "My name is Makeba."

"What a special name. I saw Miriam Makeba sing once in Nairobi. She was wonderful. And you are Chika Oke's daughter? What is your name?" she asked, pointing toward Zora.

"I'm Zora."

"Ah. Named for Zora Neale Hurston?"

"How did you know?" Zora asked.

"Because I know of your mother. I've read her two books. I know that is the kind of name she would give you. And there aren't that many Zoras around."

Mrs. Patel laughed softly and gently. "Isn't it lovely? Makeba's mother is African American and gave her the name of an African. Zora is African but has the name of an African American writer."

The girls had never thought about this. They looked at each other and smiled. In that moment, their friendship became even closer. They sat on two chairs that Mr. Patel brought in for them. Then he quietly left the room.

"So, tell me about this project and this club."

The girls excitedly told her about the Culture Club and their project. "You and your husband are both Kenyan but you look so different. We thought

all Africans looked like you, not like him. But he told us about migration."

"Good. Now let me tell you about my beloved Kenya." The girls started writing while she talked. By the time they were done, their hands hurt. After a while they stopped writing and just listened to the sweet soft voice of Mrs. Patel.

"Can we come back?" Zora asked when they saw that she was getting tired.

"Yes. I would like that," Mrs. Patel said. "But not tomorrow because I have chemotherapy."

"What's that?" Makeba asked.

"It is medicine for cancer," she replied.

"Is that what's wrong?" Zora asked quietly.

"Yes. That is what is wrong. My husband took this job here because he felt I would get better medical treatment here in the United States. So here we are."

"Can we come on Sunday afternoon?" Makeba asked.

"Yes. You can come on Sunday afternoon."

Zora and Chika had dinner with Makeba's family that night. The girls told their mothers about Mrs. Patel. The two women nodded. "You knew?" Makeba asked.

"Yes. Mr. Patel told us when he moved in."

"What can we do to help?" Zora asked.

Makeba looked serious and concerned. "We know we are just supposed to be doing our project, finding out about the people of Kenya. But we want to help."

Chika looked to Kim for the answer because Kim was the anthropologist. Kim smiled at them. "Studying a people does not mean you cannot help them."

The girls looked confused. "But Karla at the Culture Club said we should not get involved."

"Karla is learning too," Kim said. "Maybe you can teach her what you learn."

Zora looked happy now. "How can we help? Maybe bake some cookies and make her some tea? She says Kenyans love tea."

Chika smiled at her daughter. "Perhaps. You will find some way to help. I know you Afropuff girls." She put a hand up and patted one of her daughter's curly puffs. "You will find a way."

By Sunday afternoon, the girls still did not know how to help Mrs. Patel. They arrived at the Patels' apartment and were ushered straight into the bedroom. Mrs. Patel was reading a novel. "Have you read this?" she asked as they greeted her and sat on their seats.

She held up the book she was reading. *Moll Flanders* was the title of the book. They both shook their heads. "I read this when I was about your age," she said. "I love to read. Sit down, I will read you some of this chapter."

So the girls listened to her soft sing-song voice. Each word was pronounced perfectly. They stopped her and asked questions about this Moll Flanders in England. She was happy to talk about the book. Then she put it down and told them about how she met her husband. They met at college in Nairobi. They fell in love and got married, even though some people thought an African should not marry an Indian.

"Why is that?" Zora asked.

"Ah, my dear." Mrs. Patel shook her head. "Human beings are like that. They try and separate people any way they can. Sometimes they use skin color."

Makeba frowned. "I know that happens here but I just never thought it happened in Africa!"

Mrs. Patel said, "It happens everywhere in this world. But we overcame the bad talk. My husband is a good man. I am so glad I married him. I am sorry I am sick and giving him much trouble."

"I don't think he minds," Zora smiled.

Mrs. Patel smiled. "Come closer, both of you. Let me see your hair." The girls came forward and sat on the edge of her bed. Mrs. Patel's small hands patted their puffs gently. "So alike," she said. "I used to wear mine like this too. I used to love it because it made me look different. All my friends were straightening their hair and I refused to do so. Mr. Patel told me he noticed my hair first."

"Really?" said Makeba. "How do you wear it now?" She looked at Mrs. Patel's scarf.

"Ah. Now I have no hair. That is what the medicine does."

The girls were sad for her. "But it is so good to feel your hair," Mrs. Patel said as she continued to touch their puffs. "It reminds me of home. Of childhood. Of my mother. And my little Georgie has hair like his father, not like me. His hair is straight and glossy. I have missed the feel of this wonderful, rich texture."

The girls were suddenly grateful they had their afropuffs. They told Mrs. Patel about Caroline laughing at their hair. "Let her laugh. Her laughter does not harm you in any way. Maybe she wishes she had afropuffs." Makeba and Zora laughed at the idea of Caroline with afropuffs.

Mrs. Patel sat upright in bed and made a suggestion. "The afropuffs are my favorite but when you need a change, you can do two nice cornrows." She showed Makeba how to cornrow as she did Zora's hair. Then she instructed Zora to watch while she did Makeba's. She seemed to really enjoy doing it.

Then they told her about the photos from Julie. "A nice gesture," she said. "But your mother is right. I would not want to see a photo of giraffes on your board if you are studying Kenya's people. Why don't you photograph me and my family?"

"Can we?" Zora asked.

"Please?" Makeba added.

"Of course. Since this Julie likes to take photographs, ask her if she wants to come and practice on the Patels."

The girls were thrilled but doubtful that Julie would want to come since she lived next to Caroline and she probably would not want Caroline to know about this.

Then Mrs. Patel began to wilt. But she did not want them to leave so Makeba read a chapter of *Moll Flanders* to her. The two girls tip-toed out of the room when Mrs. Patel had fallen asleep.

Chapter 14:

An Afropuffs Report

On Monday, Makeba told Li to ask Julie if she wanted to come over and take photographs of the Patels for their project. "If she doesn't want to, that's OK," Makeba said. "We can do it ourselves." Li sat next to Julie in class so he would be able to pass the message along without letting Caroline know.

During recess, after a fast race in which Zora, Makeba, and Li beat Tom and two of his friends, the three friends sat on the grass and talked about Mrs. Patel. Li told the girls that he had passed the message along to Julie and she would let them know if she could do it.

Just then, Caroline, Janelle, and Julie walked up to them. Of course, Caroline had to speak. "So, what are Grumpy and Happy up to these days? Too bad you couldn't come with us to the Girl Scout party last week. It was so much fun! Still doing that *boring* project?"

"Yeah, whatever," Makeba said, rolling her eyes.

Then Julie did something unexpected. "When can I come over?" She winked at Makeba and Zora.

"How about Friday afternoon, after school?" Zora asked. Caroline and Janelle looked at Julie as if she had sprouted horns.

"Sure," Julie replied. "Do you have a computer?" Makeba nodded.

"Good. Then we can download the photos from my digital camera and print them out immediately."

Makeba said, "Perfect. So we'll have them in time for our Culture Club meeting that night. Thanks."

Julie moved off and Caroline and Janelle followed her. Makeba, Zora, and Li heard Caroline ask, "What was all *that* about?" And they heard Janelle, "How come you didn't tell us?" They smiled at Julie's confident reply, "Oh. I didn't think you two would be interested."

When it was time to gather their books and head for the bus, Mrs. Anderson stopped at the girls' desks. "How's that project going, girls?"

"Wonderful," both girls said at the same time.

"Will you share it with the class?" she asked.

The girls agreed to bring their board in. "Oh, and Mrs. Anderson," called Zora as their teacher turned back to her desk. "Have you read *Moll Flanders*?"

She shook her head. "No."

"You should read it in your book club. You'd really enjoy it."

When Julie's mother dropped Julie by Makeba's place on Friday afternoon, the girls were waiting outside. They both gasped when they saw Julie get out of the car with her small camera bag.

"Nice hairdo," said Zora, pointing to Julie's two ponytails. She had bunched her hair on top of her head so that they somehow looked like two floppy balls sitting there.

She looked shyly at the two girls. "Well, I sort of thought I would try and look like you two." Makeba did not quite know what to say so she half-smiled. They went straight to the Patels' apartment. The whole family was waiting for them.

"Ah, this is your photographer friend?" Mrs. Patel smiled at Julie. "An Afropuff girl too, I see. This hairstyle is like your uniform."

Mrs. Patel was looking nice, in a colorful dress and matching head wrap. She looked like a princess. Mr. Patel wore a jacket and tie and black pants. Georgie was in a nice t-shirt and a pair of jeans.

"How should we sit, Ms. Photographer?" Mr. Patel asked Julie. She was very excited. This was her first serious job.

Since Makeba and Zora had told her that Mrs. Patel was ill, she told Mrs. Patel to stay seated. Mr. Patel was to sit on the arm of the chair, and Manny could stand on the other side. Julie took some shots with her digital camera. Then Mrs. Patel asked Julie if she could get some shots of her with Makeba and Zora. They got lots of shots.

After Julie was done, Mr. Patel invited the girls to stay for tea. They sat with the family and chatted

and drank sweet Kenyan tea and ate crunchy coconut cookies that Mrs. Patel had made. She called them biscuits.

Then the girls thanked the Patels and got ready to leave. "You girls will come back and see me?" Mrs. Patel asked.

"Can we?" Zora asked.

"Of course. You are like my daughters. And even if this particular project ends, the learning continues."

They gently hugged Mrs. Patel and went back to Makeba's apartment. They logged onto the computer and Julie downloaded the photos. They were beautiful. Julie pulled some glossy paper from her bag and they printed out the best shots. Then, carefully, they took one photo of the Patel family and put it in the middle of their board.

The shades of the three people in the photograph went from light brown to brown to dark brown. Mrs. Patel looked gorgeous. Under the photo, Zora wrote in her best handwriting: "The People of Kenya: One Family."

Julie went with the girls to their Culture Club meeting that night. When they presented their project, everybody around the table clapped for them. Chika was there too. She had gotten out of class early and came to see what the girls presented.

Karla, who had told them not to get involved with the Patels, said, "I guess I was wrong, girls. It looks like you learned so much more about Kenya when you got to know the Patels."

"Will you try and get to know some of the people who make the Native American jewelry?" Zora asked.

"Yes. I will." Karla smiled. "Thank you, ladies."

Kim said, "I am very proud of you girls. Mr. Patel said you really brightened up things for Mrs. Patel. You are really good anthropologists because you care about the people you study."

The girls were so proud of themselves. Kim added, "And those photographs are outstanding! Good job Julie!"

"Thanks. This is such a cool club. You have fun and learn too."

"Well you're welcome to join us anytime," Kim smiled. "I see you already have some of the tools you need." She patted one of the round, floppy ponytails on Julie's head.

Everyone clapped again.

"Power to the puffs!" teased Carlos.

Two Sundays later, the girls returned to the Patels' apartment. Mr. Patel showed them into the bedroom. Zora pulled out a parcel wrapped with pink paper. She handed it to Mrs. Patel.

"What's this?" she asked.

"Open it," Makeba urged. When Mrs. Patel pulled off the paper, she uncovered a pretty framed photograph of Makeba, Zora, and herself. She wiped some tears away from her cheeks. "I am far from home and you girls have made me remember it. Thank you."

After that, the girls went to see Mrs. Patel once a week. Even when they were working on their other Culture Club projects, they would go over and talk to her about their progress. She still had to have chemotherapy for a while, but after a few weeks, she stopped and her hair started growing back. The girls, who had been practicing cornrows, waited until Mrs. Patel's hair was long enough and then they took turns braiding it for her. She loved that.

KENYA

The People of Kenya: One Family

Where it is?
East Africa, near Tanzania, Uganda, Ethiopia, Somalia, and Sudan and the Indian Ocean

How big it is:?
Twice the size of the state of Nevada

How many people?
About 34 million people

Main ethnic/people groups:
Kikuyu, Luhya, Luo, Kalenjin, Kamba, Kisii, Meru, Asian (like Mr. Patel!), European, and Arab

Languages:
English, Swahili, and others

Biggest city:
Nairobi

What Kenya sells to the world:
Tea, farming products, coffee, petroleum products, fish, and cement

Our Kenyan family:
The Patels